This Is the Way We Move

Retold by BLAKE HOENA
Illustrated by KLAUS BIPPER

CANTATA
LEARNING

WWW.CANTATALEARNING.COM

CANTATA
LEARNING

Published by Cantata Learning
1710 Roe Crest Drive
North Mankato, MN 56003
www.cantatalearning.com

Library of Congress Control Number: 2015932819
Hoena, Blake
      This Is the Way We Move / retold by Blake Hoena; Illustrated by Klaus Bipper
      Series: Tangled Tunes
      Audience: Ages: 3–8; Grades: PreK–3
      Summary: How do birds fly, elephants walk, and snakes crawl? Find out in
this twist on the classic song "This Is the Way the Ladies Ride."
      ISBN: 978-1-63290-366-2 (library binding/CD)
      ISBN: 978-1-63290-497-3 (paperback/CD)
      ISBN: 978-1-63290-527-7 (paperback)
      1. Stories in rhyme. 2. Animals—fiction. 3. Movement—fiction.

Book design and art direction, Tim Palin Creative
Editorial direction, Flat Sole Studio
Music direction, Elizabeth Draper
Music arranged and produced by Mark Oblinger

Printed in the United States of America in North Mankato, Minnesota.
122015   0326CGS16

ACCESS THE MUSIC!

SCAN
CODE
WITH
MOBILE
APP

CANTATALEARNING.COM

People move in many ways. They walk, run, skip, **jog**, and dance! Animals move in many ways, too. Some flap their wings, and others **slither**, swim, or **scurry**!

Turn the page to sing about the different ways we move!

Now here we go, singing about
the way kids move.
Watch them groove.

This is the way the children run,
jiggety-jog, jiggety-jog.

This is the way the children run,
jiggety, jiggety, jog!

Now here we go, singing about
the way birds move.
Watch them groove.

This is the way the birdies fly,
flippity-flap, flippity-flap.

This is the way the birdies fly,
flippity, flippity, flap!

Now here we go, singing about
the way elephants move.
Watch them groove.

This is the way the elephants walk,
stompety-stomp, stompety-stomp.

This is the way the elephants walk,
stompety, stompety, stomp!

Now here we go, singing about
the way snakes move.
Watch them groove.

This is the way the snakes crawl,
slithery-slide, slithery-slide.

This is the way the snakes crawl,
slithery, slithery, slide!

13

Now here we go, singing about
the way fish move.
Watch them groove.

14

This is the way the fishes swim,
swishety-swish, swishety-swish.

This is the way the fishes swim,
swishety, swishety, swish!

Now here we go, singing about
the way bugs move.
Watch them groove.

This is the way the insects creep,
clickety-click, clickety-click.

This is the way the insects creep,
clickety, clickety, click!

Now here we go, singing about
the way horses move.
Watch them groove.

This is the way the horses run,
gallop-and-**trot**, gallop-and-trot.

This is the way the horses run,
gallop and gallop and trot!

Now here we go, singing about
the way rabbits move.
Watch them groove.

This is the way the rabbits bounce,
hippity-hop, hippity-hop.

This is the way the rabbits bounce,
hippity, hippity, hop!

Now our song is done.
Wasn't that fun?

SONG LYRICS
This Is the Way We Move

Now here we go, singing about
the way kids move.
Watch them groove.

This is the way the children run,
jiggety-jog, jiggety-jog.

This is the way the children run,
jiggety, jiggety, jog!

Now here we go, singing about
the way birds move.
Watch them groove.

This is the way the birdies fly,
flippity-flap, flippity-flap.

This is the way the birdies fly,
flippity, flippity, flap!

Now here we go, singing about
the way elephants move.
Watch them groove.

This is the way the elephants walk,
stompety-stomp, stompety-stomp.

This is the way the elephants walk,
stompety, stompety, stomp!

Now here we go, singing about
the way snakes move.
Watch them groove.

This is the way the snakes crawl,
slithery-slide, slithery-slide.

This is the way the snakes crawl,
slithery, slithery, slide!

Now here we go, singing about
the way fish move.
Watch them groove.

This is the way the fishes swim,
swishety-swish, swishety-swish.

This is the way the fishes swim,
swishety, swishety, swish!

Now here we go, singing about
the way bugs move.
Watch them groove.

This is the way the insects creep,
clickety-click, clickety-click.

This is the way the insects creep,
clickety, clickety, click!

Now here we go, singing about
the way horses move.
Watch them groove.

This is the way the horses run,
gallop-and-trot, gallop-and-trot.

This is the way the horses run,
gallop and gallop and trot!

Now here we go, singing about
the way rabbits move.
Watch them groove.

This is the way the rabbits bounce,
hippity-hop, hippity-hop.

This is the way the rabbits bounce,
hippity, hippity, hop!

Now our song is done.
Wasn't that fun?

This Is the Way We Move

World
Mark Oblinger

This is the way the chil-dren run, jig-ge-ty - jog, jig-ge-ty - jog. This is the way the chil-dren run, jig-ge-ty, jig-ge-ty, jog!

Verse 2
Now here we go, singing about
the way birds move.
Watch them groove.

This is the way the birdies fly,
flippity-flap, flippity-flap.
This is the way the birdies fly,
flippity, flippity, flap!

Verse 3
Now here we go, singing about
the way elephants move.
Watch them groove.

This is the way the elephants walk,
stompety-stomp, stompety-stomp.
This is the way the elephants walk,
stompety, stompety, stomp!

Verse 4
Now here we go, singing about
the way snakes move.
Watch them groove.

This is the way the snakes crawl,
slithery-slide, slithery-slide.
This is the way the snakes crawl,
slithery, slithery, slide!

Verse 5
Now here we go, singing about
the way fish move.
Watch them groove.

This is the way the fishes swim,
swishety-swish, swishety-swish.
This is the way the fishes swim,
swishety, swishety, swish!

Verse 6
Now here we go, singing about
the way bugs move.
Watch them groove.

This is the way the insects creep,
clickety-click, clickety-click.
This is the way the insects creep,
clickety, clickety, click!

Verse 7
Now here we go, singing about
the way horses move.
Watch them groove.

This is the way the horses run,
gallop-and-trot, gallop-and-trot.
This is the way the horses run,
gallop and gallop and trot!

Verse 8
Now here we go, singing about
the way rabbits move.
Watch them groove.

This is the way the rabbits bounce,
hippity-hop, hippity-hop.
This is the way the rabbits bounce,
hippity, hippity, hop!

Outro

Now our song is done. Was-n't that fun?

GLOSSARY

gallop—to run so fast that all four of an animal's feet leave the ground at once

jog—to run at a slow pace

scurry—to hurry or run with short, quick steps

slither—to slide along by wiggling back and forth

trot—to move faster than walking but slower than jogging

GUIDED READING ACTIVITIES

1. At the beginning of the story, who goes "jiggety-jog"? Who goes "flippity-flap"? Do you remember what the other animals do?

2. Can you think of other ways animals move? What are some of the ways that you move?

3. Look at the pictures in this story and try to move like the animals do. Can you flap like a bird? Stomp like an elephant? Or slither like a snake?

TO LEARN MORE

DeMarin, Layne. *Everybody Moves*. North Mankato, MN: Capstone Press, 2012.

Guillain, Charlotte. *Bugs on the Move*. Chicago: Heinemann, 2010.

Kalman, Bobbie. *How and Why Do Animals Move?* New York: Crabtree, 2015.

Meyer, Eileen R. *Who's Faster? Animals on the Move*. Missoula, MT: Mountain Press, 2012.